Connie White Pirner

Even Little Kids
Get Diabetes

pictures by
Nadine Bernard Westcott

ALBERT WHITMAN & COMPANY
MORTON GROVE, ILLINOIS

For Lydia, my very own sugar baby. C.W.P.
For Becky. N.B.W.

Library of Congress Cataloging-in-Publication Data
Pirner, Connie White.
Even little kids get diabetes/ Connie White Pirner;
illustrated by Nadine Bernard Westcott.
p. cm.
Summary: A young girl who has had diabetes since
she was two years old describes her adjustments
to the disease.
ISBN 0-8075-2158-2
1. Diabetes in children—Juvenile literature.
[1. Diabetes.] I. Westcott, Nadine Bernard, ill. II. Title.
RJ420.D5P57 1991   90-12738
616.4'62—dc20   CIP
                                                          AC

Text © 1991 Connie White Pirner.
Illustrations © 1991 Nadine Bernard Westcott.
Designer: Karen Johnson Campbell.
Published in 1991 by Albert Whitman & Company,
6340 Oakton Street, Morton Grove, Illinois 60053.
Published simultaneously in Canada by
General Publishing, Limited, Toronto.
Printed in the United States of America.
10 9 8 7 6 5 4 3 2 1

The typeface for this book is Schneidler Medium.
The illustrations are in watercolor and ink.

I'm only a kid, but I've got diabetes.

It started when I was two years old.
I got real sick.
The doctor gave me medicine.
I didn't get better.

I was real thirsty.
I drank a lot of water.
I had to go potty a lot.
I wet my bed at night!

I got skinny,
and my ribs stuck out.
I was real hungry, too.
I felt awful!

The doctor checked me again.
He said I had diabetes.

I went to the hospital.
I was scared!

They poked my finger lots of times
to test my blood.

I cried and cried!

They put a board under my arm
and a needle into my hand.
The needle was connected to a tube.
That's how they fed me.

I got a new teddy.
Teddy got a board just like mine.

After a week, I came home.
I felt better,
but the diabetes didn't go away.

Now I'm bigger, but I still have diabetes.
I need insulin to help my body use sugar.
If I don't get insulin, I get very sick.
Sometimes I have too much insulin,
and that makes me feel shaky, hungry, and tired.
Then I have to have some juice, right away!

My finger is poked four times every day
to see if I have too much sugar
or too much insulin.

I have to have insulin shots every day.
I wipe my skin with alcohol,
and then Mommy or Daddy gives me a shot.
Someday, I'm going to do it myself.

I have to eat the right foods at the right times.
I don't ever eat candy or ice cream or cake,
not even on Halloween or at birthday parties!

I don't like shots and finger pricks,
and sometimes I want sweets real bad!

My sister thought diabetes meant I would die.
It doesn't.
It only means you have to do some special stuff
every day to stay healthy.
You have to eat the right foods at the right times.
You have to have finger pokes and shots.
If you don't do these things, you will get real sick.

But you're a regular kid.

Sometimes my mom cries because
she worries about me.
Sometimes my dad gets real mad because
I have diabetes.
I think my sister and brother don't like
me being treated special.

But Mom and Dad say it's the diabetes
they're scared of and mad at—not me.
Mom and Dad really love me.
My sister and brother do, too.
We do all this stuff so I can stay healthy
until they find a cure.

A NOTE FOR PARENTS
OF CHILDREN WHO HAVE DIABETES

Our child Lydia was two years old when she was diagnosed as having insulin-dependent diabetes. The initial shock, grief, and fear were overwhelming. We felt so alone.

I soon found out that we weren't. Over twelve million people in the United States have diabetes, and about one million of those are insulin-dependent. Half a million young people under twenty years old have insulin-dependent diabetes.

There is presently no cure for diabetes, but the disease can be managed. Parents, together with their kids who have diabetes, have to learn to plan ahead. Diet, insulin dosage, and exercise must be carefully balanced. If your child has diabetes, you will want to read and learn about the disease so you can control it as best you can. Beware of bad advice and horror stories from well-meaning people. Find a knowledgeable doctor, have a good control plan, be adaptable, and listen to your child. Don't be too hard on yourself when you mess up.

I feel that the psychological effects of diabetes can sometimes be worse than the disease itself. Encourage everyone in your family to discuss their feelings about diabetes. Try not to change your whole way of life or let your child's diabetes limit his or her activities or dreams.

We've gone through some scary times—insulin reactions, flu, getting stuck in traffic with no food. We're learning to be more prepared. We're also learning to relax.

Now, at age five, Lydia goes to kindergarten, swims, dances, spends the night away from home, and sometimes fights with her sister, Sara, and her brother, Jack. She is a busy and happy child.

Diabetes has taught me just how fragile and precious life is, not just for Lydia, but for everyone I love.

Connie White Pirner